As My Heart Awakes

As My Heart Awakes

A Waldorf Reader
for Early Third Grade

Text by Arthur M. Pittis
Illustrations by Ausa M. Peacock

Printed through support from the Norton Foundation

Title: **As My Heart Awakes**
Author: Arthur M. Pittis
Illustrator: Ausa M. Peacock
Editor: David Mitchell
Cover layout: Hallie Wootan
Proofreader: Ann Erwin
ISBN # 1-888365-62-5
© 2005 by: AWSNA Publications
             3911 Bannister Road
             Fair Oaks, CA 95628

             916-961-0927
             www.awsna.org/publications
             publications@awsna.org

   This Waldorf Reader Series is dedicated to Rosemary Gebert who was my teacher at the Waldorf Institute in 1980Ð81 and whose work as a teacher of teachers inspired me to undertake this project for the benefit of all class teachers and their students.
   The author wishes to thank the Austin Waldorf School, its teachers and students, the Waldorf Educational Foundation, the Norton Foundation, the Association of Waldorf Schools of North America, and especially David Mitchell for the support that made this reader series possible.

Printed in China

Table of Contents

John Wesley's Rule

Do all the good you can,
In all the ways you can,
In all the places you can,
At all the times you can,
To all the people you can,
As long as ever you can.

Godric and the Hare

Godric loved all living things. He planted gardens for the poor and tended each plant with love and care. One day he saw that a hare had eaten a row of ripe peas.

"She is one of God's children too and has to live," Godric said.

But the next day he saw that the hare had come back and eaten two more rows of ripe peas.

"This is too much!" Godric said. "The thief must learn a lesson."

That evening Godric waited for the hare to come back again. He did not have to wait long. Just as the moon was rising, he saw the hare slip through the garden fence.

She was careful. She stood up, looked about and carefully sniffed the air. All seemed safe. So she began to eat another row of peas.

Godric went up to her and spoke.

"I've got you now, my little thief."

The hare tried to run, but Godric was faster. He stepped in her way and picked her up. The little hare trembled as he looked her in the eye.

"I know that you are hungry, but that does not let you steal from the poor. So, what do you have to say for yourself?"

The hare could only tremble.

"Well, take this!" said Godric.

With one swift swing of his arm, he hung a ring of peas around the trembling hare's neck. Then he dropped her over the garden fence.

As she ran away Godric called, "Next time you feel hungry, don't steal from the poor. Eat the wild plants. God planted them for you."

The Ant and the Grasshopper

One warm summer day, a grasshopper sat on a blade of grass. The warm sun shone, and the warm wind danced through the grass.

"Isn't life good?" the grasshopper sang. "All I have to do is eat and sing."

Just then an ant passed by, dragging a yellow kernel of corn.

"Hey, little ant," the grasshopper called. "Why work so hard? Enjoy yourself! The sun is shining, and a warm wind dances through the grass."

The ant did not stop; she just kept dragging her yellow kernel of corn.

"Foolish grasshopper," the ant said, "don't you know winter is coming?"

"Why should I care about winter," the grasshopper said, "when I have grass to eat and songs to sing?"

"You will sing a different song when winter's here," said the ant.

"*Tra la la!*" sang the grasshopper as he danced from blade to blade of grass. "Be like me! Be like me! Enjoy your life! Don't work so hard. Have some fun!"

"You'll be sorry," said the ant, and she went on her way.

Soon the days became shorter. A cold wind blew from the north, and cold, white snow fell.

Soon the lazy grasshopper cried, "Help me! Help me, please!"

But the hard-working ant did not hear him. She was safe in her nest and had yellow corn to eat.

And so the ant lived to see the warm days of spring, but the grasshopper died of the cold.

Here We Come A-Haying

Here we come a-haying,
　A haying, a-haying,
Here we come a-haying,
　Among the leaves so green.

Up and down the mower goes
　All the long field over,
Cutting down the long green grass,
　And the purple clover.

Toss the hay and turn it,
　Laid in rows so neatly,
Summer sun a-shining down,
　Makes it smell so sweetly.

Now the farmer's ready,
   Rake it into tidy piles,
Load it on the old hay carts,
   Drawn by faithful Neddy.

Down the lane the last load goes,
   Hear the swallows calling.
Now at last our work is done,
   Night is softly falling.

— Eunice Close

The Turtle Who Talked too Much

Two geese once lived by the edge of a pond. They had made friends with a turtle who lived in the water. This turtle liked to talk, but sometimes he talked too much.

One hot summer all the water in the pond dried up.

As the geese were getting ready to fly away, one said to the other, "What about our friend the turtle? What will he do? The pond is dry, and I am afraid he will die."

Now, the two geese wanted to help their friend go to a new pond where there was water.

"We will help you go to a new pond where there is water," said one goose. "Take this stick in your beak, and we will take you with us."

"But," said the other goose, "do not talk while the stick is in your mouth. You *must* keep your mouth shut."

The turtle was happy to go with them and thanked them. He took the stick in his mouth, and they lifted him into the sky.

As they were flying high over a village, some boys and girls looked up and saw them.

"Look!" cried a girl, "Look at the silly turtle in the sky! Doesn't he know that turtles can't fly."

The turtle felt insulted, so he opened his mouth and called, "Mind your own business!"

And no sooner had he opened his mouth than he fell to his death.

"Poor turtle," said the geese. "He never knew when to keep his mouth shut."

Saint Moling and the Fox

Every morning, a fox would trot into Abbot Moling's copying room. The fox would stop at the door and look about at the monks copying books. Then he would go and sit under the abbot's desk.

Abbot Moling would stop his copying and pat the fox's head. The other monks also stopped their work. But they just rolled their eyes, as if to say, "What can we say?"

There was one monk ‑ a cranky old brother ‑ who did not like the fox. This brother worked in the hen house. He did not roll his eyes; he spoke his mind.

"Abbot Moling!" he said, "I'm happy to share God's blessing with almost any beast. But share it with a fox? That is asking too much! That fox is no good, just you wait and see."

One day the fox ran into the copying room and hid under Abbot Moling's desk. He was being chased by many angry monks. They waved sticks and shouted and shook their fists!

"Abbot Moling," shouted the cranky brother, "how can you help that thief?"

The Abbot put down his pen and looked about, "Help a thief? What do you mean?"

"That fox just stole our best hen! Look at him! Don't you see the feathers all over his chin!"

"Brother Fox," asked the abbot. "That is a very bad thing to do. What do you have to say for yourself?"

The fox just hung his head and rolled his eyes, as if to say, *"I'm sorry. I won't do it again."*

"See," said the good abbot, "Brother Fox is sorry. He has given his word; he will not do it again."

The brothers just rolled their eyes, as if to say, "What can we say?" But the cranky monk threw up his arms and said, "That fox is the devil himself. Things will get worse before they get better. Just you wait and see!"

Now the fox wanted to thank the abbot. After all, the man had saved his life. The only thing to do was to get him another hen.

Luckily, there was a farm nearby. The fox slipped into the farm-yard and took the first hen he saw. It was a big, fat one! Then he ran back to the copying room.

But as soon as he put the hen at the abbot's feet, the room filled with the farmer and many angry monks. They waved sticks and shouted and shook their fists!

"Brother Fox," said Abbot Moling, "Didn't anyone ever tell you that two wrongs don't make a right? You must give the hen back."

The farmer took his hen, looked her over and thanked the abbot. But the cranky monk just shook his head and said, "You can't make a Christian out of a beast. Its nature is too strong."

"But," said the abbot kindly, "can't you say the same about men?"

So the cranky monk just threw up his arms and went back to his hen yard.

"Well, I'm not going to wait and see," he said to himself as he began to look for holes in the fence.

℘   ℆

The next day, Abbot Moling looked down at the fox and said, "I must teach this beast how to tell the good from the bad."

So he lifted the fox onto his desk and opened a book. The fox had never looked at a book before. It looked very odd. It was white like a field of snow, and all over the white snow were little black marks.

"*What are they?*" the fox wondered. "*Ah! animal tracks!*"

"You are a smart animal," the abbot began. "This book tells about good and bad, and how the good is always the sweetest."

The man put his finger on one of the little black marks and smiled.

"*That must be good,*" thought the fox, and he licked one of the black marks. But it was not good at all; it was bitter. But then the fox saw why it was good! All around the white field of snow were little rabbits and hens.

"*So they had made the tracks! They look very good, very good . . . to eat!*"

But the best thing was the little picture of a fox. He was chasing the rabbits and hens! Now, that was the best thing of all!

But there were bad pictures too. Little men with sticks were chasing the fox. That was bad, very bad.

That night the fox wanted to know more about the good and bad, so he stole the book and took it to his den.

His pups could also see that the book was full of good things. They were so happy with it that they wanted to eat it for supper. But it tasted bitter, not like chicken or rabbit at all.

The next morning, Abbot Moling was waiting for the fox.

"Where is my book?" the abbot said as soon as the fox came into the copying room. "Bring it back now!"

So the fox ran back to his den and got the book as fast as he could.

When he put the book on the abbot's desk, he hung his head and rolled his eyes, as if to say, "*I'm sorry. I won't do it again.*"

"See," said the abbot to the other monks, "Brother Fox is sorry. He will not steal another book."

The monks just rolled their eyes, as if to say, "What can we say?"

But the cranky monk threw up his arms and went right back to his hen yard. He knew what to do — look for more holes in the fence.

Now, it is true that the fox never stole another book or another hen. Abbot Moling was right about that. But that very evening, he did steal a beehive from the garden.

As he and his pups licked the last sweet drops of honey from their paws, the fox purred, as if to say, "*The man was right. The sweetest things are always the best things of all.*"

The Boy and the Nuts

A boy once found a pitcher full of nuts, so he put his hand into the pitcher and grabbed a fist full of nuts.

But when he tried to pull his hand out, he found that the pitcher's neck was too narrow.

The boy did not know what to do. He did not want to let go of the nuts and lose them, but he did not want to keep his hand in the pitcher.

So he burst into tears.

Just then a good old woman passed by. She felt sorry for the boy.

"Why all the tears, little one?" the good woman asked.

The boy pointed at his fist and cried, "I want those nuts, but I can't get them out!"

"Silly boy," the good woman laughed, "if you could be happy with half of what you have grabbed, you would have all that you need."

Harvest Song

The boughs do shake and the bells do ring,
So merrily comes our harvest in,
Our harvest in, our harvest in,
So merrily comes our harvest in.

We have ploughed; we have sowed;
We have reaped; we have mowed;
We have brought home every load,
Hip, hip, hip harvest home!

— Traditional

The Fox and the Grapes

One day a red fox was walking through the forest. He came upon a grape vine hanging in a tree. The big blue grapes looked very good.

"Those big blue grapes will make a good lunch," the red fox thought. So he stood up on his hind legs and tried to reach them.

But the grapes were beyond his reach. He tried, and he tried, again and again. He even jumped and snapped at them with his jaws. But the blue grapes were far out of his reach.

At last, the red fox gave up.

"Who wants those grapes anyway?" he said. "They're probably sour."

A Lesson in Compassion

There once was an old monk who wanted to find deep wisdom. He meditated on a rock near a pond.

But each day as he sat down on the rock to meditate, he would see some little insect, splashing helplessly in the water.

The insect's distress would upset him deeply. So he would stop his meditations, reach down and help the insect out of the water. After he had put the little insect safely on the rock, he would begin his meditations again.

But no sooner had he begun than he would see another little insect, splashing helplessly in the water.

Once again he would stop his meditations, reach down and help the little insect out of the water.

This happened time after time and day after day.

His fellow monks saw him hopping up and down and became deeply upset.

"It is good and wise," they said, "for our master to show kindness to even the smallest creature, but how can he find deep wisdom if he is hopping up and down all day?"

So they went to him and asked, "Master, how can you meditate and find deep wisdom if you are hopping up and down all day?"

The wise old monk sat silently for a long time. Then he spoke.

"You are right. My meditation would be deeper if I sat still all day. But how can I sit still while even the smallest of God's creatures suffers distress at my feet?"

The Wolf and the Watchdog

A wolf and a watchdog met one night. The wolf was so lean and hungry that he felt near death. The dog, on the other hand, was well fed.

"Why is it, cousin," asked the wolf, "that you get so much to eat? Are you really such a better hunter?"

"Why, it's really very easy," said the dog. "If you had work like mine, you could eat as much as you wanted."

"Well, I'm ready to do almost any work if it will keep me from starving," said the wolf. "What is your work?"

"I'm a watchdog for a farmer. All I have to do is sleep at my master's door and bark if I hear a noise."

"I could do that!" said the wolf. "Let me come with you, and I'll start work right away."

As they walked back to the farm-house, the wolf saw something odd around the dog's neck.

"Cousin," the wolf asked, "what is that on your neck?"

"Oh, it's my collar."

"But what is a collar, and what is it for?"

"It's where my master hooks my chain."

"A chain!" cried the wolf, stopping. "Does that mean you are not free?"

"Well, it's not really too bad. My master only chains me during the day, but he always sets me free at night. It's a small price to pay for all you can eat."

"No, thank you, cousin," said the wolf, turning to go. "I would rather be free and starve than a fat slave on a chain."

The Miller Who Tried to Please Everybody

There once was a miller who tried to please everybody. One day he said to his boy, "How about going to market?"

The boy liked the idea, so they put some sacks of flour on their donkey's back and set off for market.

After a while, they passed three women sitting in a doorway. One of the women looked at the miller and shook her head.

"Well, look at that!" the woman said. "Did you ever see such a thing? If that man was a good father, he'd let his poor boy ride."

The miller was upset by the woman's words and said, "Well, how about that!"

So he told his boy to ride on the donkey's back.

After a while, they passed some old men sitting in the shade. One of the old men looked at the boy riding on the donkey's back and shook his head.

"Well, look at that!" he said. "It's just like I said: boys these days have no respect. If that boy was a good boy, he'd let his old father ride."

The miller was upset by the old man's words and said, "Well, how about that!"

So he climbed up on the donkey's back and rode behind the boy.

After a while, they passed some girls sitting by a well. One of the girls looked at the two riders and shook her head.

"Just look at that!" she said. "Poor donkey! Those two brutes are breaking her back. If they were good people, they'd let the poor donkey ride."

The miller was upset by the girl's words and said, "Well, how about that!"

So he and the boy climbed off the donkey's back and stood in the road for a long, long time. The miller did not know what to do.

"I know how to please everybody, Father!" said the boy. "Let's get a pole and tie the donkey to it. Then the donkey can ride!"

"Well, how about that!" said the miller. "Haven't I always said you were smart! Everybody will be pleased by that!"

So they found a pole and tied the donkey to it. It was hard work carrying the donkey between them.

After a while, they came to a bridge over a stream. Across the stream was the market where a great many people were gathered.

"Just look at that!" somebody laughed, looking at the miller and his boy carrying the donkey between them.

"Have you ever seen such a thing? Those two fools are breaking their backs giving some donkey a ride."

Everybody ran to the stream, laughing and pointing and shouting advice.

Now the donkey, who was already upset by being carried upside down, became even more upset at all the laughing and shouting.

It twisted and turned. It brayed, and it kicked. And at last, it broke free, knocking the miller and his boy into the stream.

"Well, how about that!" said the miller to his boy as they watched the donkey run away. "Who's pleased by that?"

The Boy Bishop

A long time ago, a merchant and his good wife were blessed with all the good things in life except a child. So they prayed to God and gave gifts to the poor. At last, God gave them a baby boy. They called him Nicolas, which means victorious.

As the servants washed the newborn baby, he stood up in his tub and spoke. The women were very afraid.

"The child is cursed! The devil has him!" they cried and ran away.

The next day was Friday, and the boy would not nurse. His mother felt afraid.

"Maybe the devil *does* have the boy." she wondered.

So she prayed to God, and by the next day all was well.

A week passed, and on the next Friday, the baby would not nurse again. Now his mother looked down at him and asked, "Is my milk bad?"

The baby looked up at her and spoke. "Friday is God's fast day. It is God's law that we should not eat."

Then his mother was full of joy, for she felt in her heart that the boy would grow up to be a holy man.

⸏   ⸎

When Nicolas was nine years old, a great sickness struck his land. Many died of the sickness, even his parents. He was now alone in the world, so he set out by himself.

One day he came to a city where the bishop also had died of the sickness. All the other bishops in the land had come to the city to elect a new bishop.

That night the leader of the bishops had a dream. In his dream an angel told him, "Let Nicolas be the one." The next morning he told the other bishops about his dream.

"Let Nicolas come forward," the leader of the bishops proclaimed. But no one moved. No one there was named Nicolas.

Just then the door opened. All the bishops turned and glared at the boy who stood in the door.

"How dare you come in here!" one of the bishops said.

"Go away, boy!" said another.

"Who do you think you are?" said a third bishop.

"My name is Nicolas; God has sent me here because my parents are dead."

The bishops were amazed.

"This is a miracle!" their leader said. "Here is the one of whom the angel told me."

So they made the boy their new bishop.

As they led Nicolas out of the church, all the city cheered. But the devil, who was watching, was filled with envy and rage.

"I will spoil their joy," the evil one swore.

As Nicolas passed down the street, the devil saw a boy who was standing by the side of a well. He slipped up behind the boy and pushed him in.

As the boy fell, Nicolas felt the boy's fear and lifted three fingers into the air. At once, the boy stopped falling and flew out of the well.

"I'm saved!" the boy cried.

"A miracle! A miracle!" everyone cheered.

But the devil did not cheer. He could only snarl and storm away.

"From now on," the evil one swore, "that Nicolas is my special enemy."

And thus did Nicolas become the patron saint of children and the special enemy of the devil.

The Gnat and the Lion

A gnat once flew up to a lion and buzzed about his head.

"You think you're the strongest beast, don't you?" the gnat mocked.

"Of course," said the lion. "I am the King of the Beasts."

"Well," mocked the gnat. "Let's fight, and I'll prove you wrong."

The gnat sounded his mighty hum and the lion his mighty roar. The gnat flew right at the lion and stung him on his nose. The lion swung his sharp claws but only scraped his own nose. Finally, the lion fell down, too tired to fight any more.

"See!" boasted the gnat. "There you lie, bleeding to death while I buzz my mighty hum. Now who's the strongest of beasts?"

The proud gnat flew off but did not fly far. He flew right into a spider's web.

As the spider crept towards him, the gnat cried, "How unfair! Why must I, the strongest of beasts, be dinner for a mere spider?"

Jack Frost Was in the Garden

Jack Frost was in the garden;
I saw him there at dawn;
He was dancing round the bushes
And prancing on the lawn.
He had a cloak of silver,
A hat all shimm'ring white,
A wand of glittering star-dust,
And shoes of sunbeam light.

Jack Frost was in the garden,
When I went out to play.
He nipped my toes and fingers
And quickly ran away.
I chased him round the wood-shed,
But, oh! I'm sad to say
That though I chased him everywhere,
He simply wouldn't stay.

Jack Frost was in the garden
But now I'd like to know
Where I can find him hiding;
I've hunted high and low –
I've lost his cloak of silver,
His hat all shimm'ring white,
His wand of glittering star-dust,
His shoes of sunbeam light.

– *John P. Smeeton*

Bell the Cat

There was once a barn full of mice. Day and night, a cat hunted them down and ate them up. One night when the cat was away, the mice held a meeting.

"Something must be done about that cat," squeaked a mother mouse. "She ate my family."

"Hear, hear!" squeaked a second mouse. "That cat is the very devil."

"Nobody's safe while she's around," squeaked a third mouse.

Just then a bold, young mouse jumped up and squeaked, "We need to stand up to that cat! I'm sick and tired of being pushed around!"

"Hear, hear!" squeaked the other young mice, twitching their whiskers boldly.

One bold, young mouse even jumped on top of a hay bale and squeaked, "Death to all cats! Long live the mice!"

"To war! To war!" all the young mice squeaked. Some ran up the walls and some ran down.

They seemed so brave and squeaked and chattered their teeth so loudly that all the other mice wanted war too.

"Fools!" squeaked one of the mother mice. "Do you think war will save us? You talk big, but the cat is bigger. She will eat you for sure. We need to find a better way than war."

"I know!" squeaked her son, a little mouse who liked to chew on the farmer's books. "Let's put a bell on the cat. Then we'll hear her coming."

"That's my boy!" the mother mouse squeaked. "Didn't I tell you he was the smartest mouse of all?"

The mice were now very happy. They danced about the barn,

jumping from hay bale to hay bale and running up and down the walls wildly.

The smart little mouse even found a little bell and dragged it out for all the mice to see. As the mice stood looking at it, they squeaked about how good life would be now.

"Friends, there is just one problem," squeaked the oldest and wisest mouse of all.

Everyone looked at him and wondered what he would say.

"Tell me," he squeaked wisely, "who will bell the cat?"

The Three Dowerless Maidens

There once was a selfish man who loved gold more than he loved his own daughters. One day he went to a wicked woman and said, "I do not like being poor. Will you buy my oldest daughter?"

"Why should I buy her?" asked the wicked woman. "Tell me what you will do with the money."

"I will use some of the gold as a dowry for the next girl and spend the rest on myself," said the selfish man.

The old woman liked his plan and said, "Bring the girl to me, and I'll give you a sack of gold."

That night the man said to his oldest daughter, "Make ready, my child. Tomorrow we will go on a trip. We will see many wonderful sights."

The girl was happy. She thanked her father and packed up the few things she had in this world and went to bed.

No sooner had she fallen asleep than she heard a voice.

"Beware, dear child. Your father plans to sell you to a wicked woman and use the money as a dowry for your sister. In your stocking you will find a sack of gold. Make him use it for your dowry, and you will be saved."

In the morning when the girl awoke, she was very afraid.

"What a terrible nightmare" she thought. "I'm glad it was only a dream."

But when she pulled on her stocking and found the gold, she knew the voice had spoken the truth.

She went to her father.

"Here," she said, "is gold for my dowry. Now find me a husband."

The selfish man had to obey, and so the first daughter was saved.

When the selfish man's second daughter came of age, he went to the wicked old woman and sold the girl for a sack of gold.

"Now," he said, "I'll have a dowry for my third daughter, and I will spend the rest on myself."

He went to his second daughter and said, "Make ready, my child. Tomorrow we go on a trip. We will see many wonderful sights."

The girl was happy. She thanked her father and packed up the few things she had in this world and went to bed.

No sooner had she fallen asleep than she too heard a voice.

"Beware, dear child. Your father plans to sell you to a wicked woman and use the money as a dowry for your sister. In your stocking you will find a sack of gold. Make him use it for your dowry, and you will be saved."

In the morning, the second daughter awoke, trembling from head to toe.

"What a terrible nightmare" she thought. "I'm glad it was only a dream."

But when she pulled on her stocking and found the gold, she knew the voice had spoken the truth.

She went to her father.

"Here," she said, "is gold for my dowry. Now find me a husband."

The selfish man had to obey, and so the second daughter was saved. But he was as poor as before.

෨   ൙

Now, his third daughter was the most beautiful girl of all. But he could find no one who would marry a poor girl without a dowry.

Everyone said the same thing, "A girl without a dowry is like a spring without rain."

So the man went back to the wicked woman.

"You again," she laughed. "Isn't this one your last girl?"

Her voice made him afraid, so he acted bravely.

"This time, no-one will trick me out of my gold," he bragged. "I'll hide in her room and catch any thief who comes in the night."

"My!" said the wicked woman, "you are a brave one. Here is your gold."

So the selfish father went to his third daughter and said, "Make ready, my child. Tomorrow we go on a trip to see many wonderful sights."

The girl was happy. She thanked her father, packed the few things she had in this world, then jumped into bed.

When the girl was fast asleep, the father crept into her room. He sat in the shadows and watched as the hours passed. At last, dawn brightened the sky.

"Ah, now I am safe," he sighed and fell asleep. But something woke him; and as he awoke, he saw someone jump out the window.

"Stop thief! What have you done to my girl?"

He chased the thief across the yard. But when he grabbed the thief, he saw that it was the boy bishop, Nicolas.

"Forgive me, good Bishop," the man cried, and he dropped to his knees. "I now see how I've sinned."

"It is not for me to forgive you," replied Nicolas. "Only God and your daughters can do that."

From then on, the poor man had to make his own living. Whether his three daughters ever forgave him, the story does not say. You will have to find the answer in your own heart. But now you know why children in Christian lands hang stockings on Christmas Eve.

The Frog in the Pail of Cream

Two frogs were hopping around a barn when they hopped right into a pail of cream. Try as they might, they could not hop out.

One of the frogs lost hope and let himself drown. But the other frog was no quitter. He kicked, and he swam, hour after hour.

Just as he was feeling weak, he felt the cream getting firm. All his kicking and swimming had churned the cream into a chunk of butter.

He climbed up on top of the chunk of butter and saw that he was now high enough to hop out. And he did!

The Witch

I saw her plucking cowslips,
    And marked her where she stood:
She never knew I watched her
    While hiding in the wood.

Her skirt was brightest crimson,
    And black her steeple hat,
Her broomstick lay beside her –
    I'm positive of that.

Her chin was sharp and pointed,
    Her eyes were – I don't know –
For, when she turned towards me –
    I thought it best to go!

– Percy H. Hott

The Banyan Deer

There once was a deer the color of gold. His eyes were like jewels. His antlers were white as silver. His mouth was red as a rose, and his hoofs were hard and bright. He was a king of the forest and ruled a herd of five hundred Banyan deer.

Also living in the same forest was a herd of Monkey deer. They were smaller than the Banyan, and their king was not as fine.

Now the human King of this land loved to eat deer meat. Each day, he sent his hunters into the forest to hunt the deer. To make the hunters' work easier, he ordered villagers to stop their work and drive the deer to them.

Because of the King's order, the villagers never got any work done, so they decided to build a hunting park for their King.

Once the park was done, the villagers drove the two herds of deer into it and shut the gate. Now the hunters could find as many deer as they liked, and the villagers could do their work.

One day, the King came to see the hunting park. As the villagers were showing it to him, the King saw the two deer kings.

"Those two deer are kings of the forest," he said to his hunters. "I grant them their lives. You may not hunt them, but you may hunt as many of the other deer as you like."

So the King's hunters hunted the herds easily, killing a great many of them. One day, the Banyan Deer King spoke with the Monkey Deer King.

"It is now too easy for the hunters. They are killing more of our brothers and sisters than ever before. Soon our herds will be no more."

"What shall we do?" asked the Monkey Deer King.

"Let me send one of my herd on the first day. Then on the next day, you send one of your herd. In this way the hunters will kill only the deer we send them, and our herds will be saved."

"That is fair," said the Monkey Deer King. "You are wise, indeed."

So first one deer from the Banyan herd gave up its life, and then one deer of the Monkey herd did the same.

One day, a mother deer of the Monkey herd was called to give up her life, so she went to her king.

"Oh, Monkey Deer King," she begged her king, "please send another in my place. My fawn is so little, and she cannot live without me. If I die, she will die too. When she no longer needs me, I will go."

But her king would not help her.

"It is the law," he said. "You must go."

She next went to the Banyan Deer King and begged him to save her life.

"Go back to your fawn. I will take your place," said the noble Banyan Deer King.

When the hunters found the Banyan King waiting at the gate to be killed, they were afraid and ran back to their King and asked what they should do.

When their King heard that the Banyan Deer King waited at the gate, he himself went back with his hunters.

"King of the Banyan," the King asked, "why are you here? I granted you your life."

"Yes, you did. But a mother deer came to me and begged me to spare her life so her fawn might live. It would be wrong to order another to take her place, so I came myself."

"Noble king of the forest," said the human King, "never before have I seen such kindness. Your life is spared, and never again will my hunters kill any deer."

The Jackass in the Lion's Skin

Once a jackass came upon a lion's skin. It was hanging on a wall. Hunters had hung it there to dry, but the jackass felt it had been left for him.

"Wouldn't I look fearsome in that!" he brayed.

So he put the lion's skin over his back and went on his way.

Soon he came to his own barnyard. When everyone saw him, they were very afraid. The people ran into their houses, and the animals ran into the barn.

The jackass was now very happy with himself, so he squatted down in the mud and let out a proud bray.

"He Haw! Hee Haaww! Heee Haaawww!"

All this braying woke an old dog who was sleeping in the sun.

"Fool," she barked, "do you think fine clothes hide the fact that you are really just an ass?"

The Three Schoolboys and the Salting Tub

One morning three boys set off for school. It was a fine spring day.

"Why waste such a day in school?" said one of the boys. "We could go for a swim."

"Or we could climb up the mountain and watch the ships out at sea."

"Or better yet," said the oldest, "we could climb over the mountain and visit my uncle. He has a fine horse!"

The other two boys liked this idea, so they hid their books in a hollow tree and set off.

Higher and higher, they climbed until the houses below them looked like little toys. Half way up the mountain, they stopped to eat lunch. The blue sky and ocean sparkled brightly as far as they could see.

"How far is it?" asked the youngest.

"Oh, not very far," said the oldest.

Higher and higher they climbed. Hours passed, and the path became steep and hard.

But the boys felt brave.

Finally, a stiff wind began to blow. The sky grew black, and the boys became afraid.

"Please, let's turn back," said the youngest boy.

"And miss riding that fine horse?" said the oldest. "It's not very far."

But the sky grew blacker.

Soon the wind began to howl, and cold rain soaked them to the bone.

The path was now too dark to follow easily, so they took hands. Trembling with fear, they pushed on.

After a while, they saw two dim red lights in the distance.

"It's the eyes of a devil!" cried the youngest boy.

"No, no," the oldest one comforted him."It is only a house!"

"Then we are saved," said the third.

Soon they came to a broken-down hut. Its roof over-hung the dim red windows like a frowning brow. There was an evil feeling

about the house, and they did not want to go near.

But the boys were colder than afraid, so they tapped on the dark door. It swung open, and there stood a fearsome man. In his hand, he held a steaming ladle.

"Come in, my dear boys," he said in a sweet, friendly voice.

"Thank you, sir," they said as they crept through the door.

"Come sit by the fire while I make you some warm soup and a nice, soft bed."

They sat by the fire and shared some warm soup. Then their host tucked them into a nice, warm bed.

But no sooner were they asleep than the wicked host killed them and put them into a big salting tub that he used to cure meat.

Seven years passed.

One day Bishop Nicolas was climbing up that same mountain path. At dusk, he found himself in front of the old, low-roofed hut. A storm was brewing, so he tapped on the door.

"Come in, Bishop Nicolas," called a sweet, friendly voice. "Come in and enjoy some warm soup and a nice, soft bed."

Now the wicked man thought he would spite the good bishop by giving him a special treat. As he opened the salting tub, the bishop lifted three fingers into the air.

"Come out, my dear boys," Nicolas called.

Instantly, the lid of the salting tub flew out of the wicked man's hand, and the three boys hopped out, as happy and well as the day they left home.

"My, I slept well!" said the oldest boy.

"And so did I!" said the second

"Me too!" laughed the youngest of all. "I even dreamed we were in Paradise."

The wicked host, who was really the devil, howled bitterly and stormed off into the night.

Since then Saint Nicolas has been known as the patron saint of school children – the naughty as well as the nice.

The Lion and the Mouse

One fine day some playful mice found a lion napping in the forest. They ran up his back and slid down his nose.

All this running up and sliding down upset the lion's napping, so he opened one eye.

"Ah!" he said and trapped one of the mice under his paw.

"Please don't kill me," the mouse begged. "If you spare my life, I'll repay you in kind some day."

"A little mouse help me?" laughed the lion. "Be gone and don't bother me again."

He let the little mouse go and fell back asleep.

Later that day, the lion set off for his den. But while he had been napping, some hunters had laid a net across his path.

As he passed, he sprang the trap and was swung up into the air and caught.

Hard as he tried, the lion could not free himself. Just then, the mouse hopped out and began gnawing at the ropes. Soon the lion was able to pull himself free.

"Thank you, little friend," said the lion.

"Didn't I say I would help you some day?" said the mouse. "After all, one good deed always deserves another."

The Miser

A miser once sold everything he had and bought a lump of gold. He loved this lump of gold and buried it deep in the forest. Every night he slipped into the forest, dug up his gold and admired it.

One night a thief followed him. The thief watched the miser carefully. Then after the miser had left, the thief dug up the gold and stole it.

When the miser found his gold stolen, he wept so bitterly that a nearby hermit heard him.

"Why are you weeping so bitterly?" asked the hermit.

"My gold! It's gone! Someone stole it!" The miser then told his story.

"Friend," said the hermit, "take this stone and bury it. It will bring you the same profit."

"How can a mere stone bring me any profit?" wept the miser.

"How did your gold, when it was buried in the forest, bring you any more profit?"

Two Little Kittens

Two little kittens, one stormy night,
Began to quarrel, and then to fight.

One had a mouse, and the other had none,
And that's the way a quarrel's begun.

"I'll have that mouse," said the bigger cat.
"You'll have this mouse? We'll see about that!"

"I'll have that mouse," said the oldest one.
"This mouse is mine!" said the youngest one.

I told you before 'twas a stormy night
When these two kittens began to fight.

Their mistress seized her sweeping broom,
And swept those kittens right out of the room.

The ground was covered with frost and snow,
And the two little kittens had nowhere to go.

So they lay right down before the door
Until their mistress let them in once more.

Then in they crept, as quiet as mice,
All wet with the snow and cold as ice.

They found it better on a stormy night,
To curl up together than quarrel and fight.

— *Anonymous*

The Golden Cups

There once was a vain man who had many daughters but not one son. Every night he knelt before an image of Saint Nicolas and prayed.

"Good Saint, if you give me a son, I will give your church a cup of the finest gold."

As if in reply to his prayers, a son was born, and the vain man was filled with happiness and pride.

"See what my prayers have done?" he boasted. "Now I will do as I said."

So without delay, the man went to the best goldsmith in the land.

"Spare no cost, but make me a gold cup that is the finest cup in the world!"

The goldsmith worked for two full years. When the cup was finished, it was the finest cup the vain man had ever seen.

Its stem was shaped like two angels with wings lifted in praise. Its bowl was inlaid with the purest pearls that looked like grapes ready to be pressed into wine.

Then the vain man thought, "This cup is too beautiful to give away. I'll make a second cup, a smaller one for the saint's gift. After all, who will ever know?"

When the second, smaller cup was done, the vain man was very pleased, and he set out for Saint Nicolas' church, taking his son with him. But while at sea, a wave swept the boy off the boat.

The man wept and pulled his hair.

"A chest of gold for the man who saves my boy!" he cried.

But the child could not be found.

When the vain man arrived at the church, he placed the second, smaller cup upon the altar. But it fell onto the floor with a hollow ring. He picked it up and put it back, but again it fell.

He tried over and over again.

"What could be wrong?" he wondered.

He turned the cup over, but the bottom was flat. So he tried one more time, but once again it fell with a hollow ring.

When the vain man arrived home, he took out the first cup and gazed on it. Surely, it was the most beautiful cup he had ever seen. But he felt no joy in its beauty. He felt only sorrow and pain.

ଚ   ଡ

Months passed. Every day, the man took out the two golden cups and gazed at them. Finally, he understood. These cups were made for God.

He packed his bag. But when he was all set to go, there was something he had to do first. Many times, he tried to go, but each time he stayed, and so the years passed.

Hard times befell the man. He grew old and bitter. His wife no longer loved him, and she moved away with his daughters.

Finally, he became so poor that he had to borrow money. Then he had to sell the last things he had to pay back his loans.

Only the two golden cups were left of all his riches, but he would not sell them.

One day the goldsmith came to his door.

"I know a rich man who wants to buy your golden cups. He will give you a good price for them."

"No, I will not sell them. They are the saint's."

"Do not be a fool, man. His price is the best you will ever get. What will the saint ever give you for them?"

"No, I will not sell them."

"Then don't blame me if you starve," said the goldsmith as he left.

That afternoon the man put the two golden cups in a sack and left home. The trip was long and hard. As he watched the waves roll across the sea, he remembered his son and wept for the long lost boy.

As soon as he landed, he went to Saint Nicolas' church. First, he placed the smaller cup on the altar. It fell to the floor.

"Ah," he murmured.

Then he took out the bigger cup—the finest cup in the world—and placed it on the altar.

It did not move.

"Ah," he murmured.

After picking up the smaller cup, he turned to go. An old man was walking towards him. The man wore a bishop's robe and had kind, grey eyes. He was leading a little boy by the hand.

"How can this be?" the man gasped. "My son? Is it you?"

The old man in the bishop's robe smiled kindly and gave him the boy's hand. Then the grey-eyed man looked at the cup in his hand and nodded towards the altar.

"Ah," the vain man murmured, and he did what he had to do. He put the second cup next to the first.

This time, the cup did not fall.

The Chimp and the Dolphin

A chimp went to sea with his master, a rich merchant. One day the chimp was swinging on the boat's ropes and fell into the sea. But luckily for him, a dolphin saved his life.

As the dolphin was carrying the chimp to shore, the chimp began to brag.

"I'm a rich merchant, you know. I have four feet of coins and two gallons of servants. When I get home, I'll throw ten inches into the water for you."

The dolphin had never before met a rich merchant, so she did not know what to think.

"And let me tell you," the chimp bragged, "I can count to twenty and even fourteen. Not many merchants can do that! Most of the ones I know can only count to a hundred. I bet you can't do twice that?"

"I don't know anything about counting," said the dolphin. "I never went to school. I went to sea the day I was born."

"I pity you," laughed the chimp. "It is hard being foolish."

By now the dolphin was feeling glad that they were nearing shore. The chimp was becoming a burden.

"I'll take you to those rocks," the dolphin said. "From there I'm sure you can find your way home."

"Weigh home?" declared the chimp. "I know how to weigh homes. I'd say those rocks will make a very good home and weigh about ten feet each. Why, I could weigh those rocks minus the ocean in my five hands."

"Faker!" cried the dolphin who now knew the chimp for what he was. With a flip of her tail, she dove under the waves, and the chimp had to save himself.

The Dog and the Porcupine

A long time ago, the dog and the porcupine were friends. The dog was easy-going and liked to help everybody. The porcupine was . . . let us say . . . prickly.

One day the porcupine came to the dog's house.

"Friend," said the porcupine, "I have no house and must live in the bush all day and night. It's not very nice out there, so help me out."

"Of course," said the dog, and he invited the porcupine to live with him.

The dog gave the porcupine food and a bed. The next morning the dog showed the porcupine some fat, green sticks.

"Do you know what these are?" asked the dog.

"Of course not. I live in the bush and eat grass. How would I know what anything is?"

"It is sugar cane. Try some. It is very sweet."

So the porcupine tried the sugar cane and liked it a lot.

"How can I get more?" the porcupine asked.

"Go into my field and take what you need, but don't eat the roots. If you eat the roots no more sugar cane will grow."

But the porcupine paid the dog no mind. He dug up the sugar cane, roots and all, until nothing was left.

When the dog saw what the porcupine had done, he spoke to him.

"I thought you were my friend, but you went into my field and dug up the sugar cane, roots and all, until nothing was left."

"Your field?" huffed the porcupine. "Why, that field is as much mine as it is yours."

The easy-going dog was surprised and did not know what to say.

                                                  ℘   ℛ

The next morning the porcupine went to another animal's field. He dug up the sugar cane, roots and all, until nothing was left.

Day after day, he did the same thing until he went into the human's field and dug up the sugar cane, roots and all, until nothing was left.

The humans blamed the animals and began to chase them with spears.

"Why are the humans so angry?" asked all the animals. "What have we done wrong?"

"It's the dog's fault," said the porcupine. "He dug up their sugar cane, roots and all, until nothing was left."

"Foolish dog!" the animals cried. "How could he do such a thing?"

So they went to the dog's house.

"Dog! Come out here right now."

The easy-going dog came out and asked, "Why are you so angry? Is something wrong?"

"You're a bad dog. You dug up the humans' sugar cane, roots and all, until nothing was left. Now they chase us with spears."

"No!" said the dog. "I didn't do that. It was the porcupine."

"Oh!" cried the porcupine. "What a liar! You know you dug up the sugar cane, roots and all, until nothing was left."

"This isn't fair," said the dog. "I want to go before a judge and clear my good name."

All the animals agreed that they would take the dog's case before the judge the very next morning.

℘   ℭ

Early the next morning the porcupine woke the dog up.

"Hurry up, lazy bones," poked the porcupine. "You don't want to be late before the judge."

"But it's still black night," whined the dog. "Let's wait until dawn."

"No," insisted the porcupine. "We must go now."

So the easy-going dog agreed.

Blackness was everywhere, and the air was very damp and cold. The dog started to shiver and whine, but the porcupine did not feel a thing. After a while, the porcupine left the path and went into the tall grass.

"Why can't we stay on the path?" whined the dog. "The grass is so wet."

"We're going through the grass," insisted the porcupine. "Now hurry up, or you'll be late. That wouldn't look good with the judge."

So the easy-going dog agreed.

They went through the wet grass. Mile after mile, they went. The dog became very cold and shivered so much that his teeth rattled, but the porcupine did not feel a thing.

When they arrived at the judge, the sun was already high in the sky. All the animals were waiting. They had been there since dawn.

"You are late. Where have you been?" they asked.

"The dog is to blame," said the

porcupine. "He ran off into the tall grass, and I had to find him."

The judge called the dog to him.

"Stand here before me," the judge said. "Did you dig up the sugar cane, roots and all, until nothing was left?"

The poor dog was terribly cold. He just stood before the judge and shivered. He shivered so much that his teeth almost rattled out of his head.

"Look at him," said the porcupine. "See how he shivers and rattles his teeth in fear before the judge. He acts like he's guilty."

"Yes," all the animals agreed. "He acts like he's guilty."

"Well, dog," asked the judge, "have you nothing better to say for yourself?"

But the dog's teeth rattled so much that all he could say was, "Chh, chh, chh, chh!"

"So you have nothing to say for yourself?" the judge asked.

But the dog could only shiver and
rattle and said, "Chh, chh, chh, chh, chh!"

"Then, dog, I find you guilty," declared
the judge. "You cannot be trusted. From
this day onward, you will have to be
chained."

So there, my friends, is why the dog
spends his days chained. Oh, yes! It
also tells us why he barks at all the other
animals when they pass by.

The Suspicious Disciple

One day a young disciple saw Master Rumi carrying a tray of fine food through the streets of the city.

"How can Master Rumi eat such fine food? Hasn't he sworn to live a simple life?" the disciple wondered. "Hasn't he told us that fine food like that is only for rich men who think only of themselves and not of others?"

The disciple was very upset.

"Could our master have a false heart?" he wondered. "Is he sneaking away to eat that food where no one will see him?"

Now the disciple needed to know if Master Rumi was the kind of man who said one thing but did another. So he decided to follow his master to see if he was sneaking away to eat the rich food in secret.

The disciple followed Master Rumi through the city's streets and out the city gate. He then followed his master through some woods and across a field. At last, the master went into an old farm house. The disciple slipped up to the house and peeked in the window.

There sat Rumi on the floor. Beside him lay a mother dog and her four new pups. Rumi was feeding the mother the rich food, and she was nursing her puppies.

Then Master Rumi felt his disciple's eyes on him. He looked up and put his fingers to his lips.

"You know your heart is awake," he whispered, "when you can hear soft cries for help from miles away."

At the Lion's Den

Once there was a lion who became too old to hunt. Instead of starving, he acted like he was ill. He lay deep in his cave and moaned as if he were near death.

When the other animals heard of the lion's illness, they came to see him. Some were sorry that their king was dying, and some were just curious. Some were glad that the old killer would soon be gone and came to gloat.

One by one, the animals went into the cave, and the old lion ate them. So despite his age, he was better off than before.

Only the fox stayed outside.

"How goes it, my king?" called the fox from the mouth of the cave.

"Not well, not well," moaned the lion. "I'm nearly blind. Come a little closer, my friend, so I can see you one last time."

"If you'll excuse me, my king, I'd rather stay outside. I can see many tracks going into your den, but none coming out."

Why the Dog and the Cat Are Enemies

There once was a man and his wife who owned a golden ring. The ring was a lucky ring, and whoever owned it had everthing they would ever need.

Sad to say, the man and woman did not know that the ring was lucky, and one day they sold it to a rich man. As soon as the ring was gone, they became poor, and the man who bought it became richer.

Now, the man and woman had a dog and a cat. These two creatures suffered with them.

Luckily, the dog knew the secret of the ring, and one day he said to the cat, "Long Whiskers, we must get the ring back."

"But how, Waggy Tail?" asked the cat. "The ring is at the rich man's house, and he keeps it in a wooden box that he locks with a key."

"You must catch a mouse," said the dog. "Tell the mouse that if she gnaws a hole in the box, you will not eat her."

"You are a smart one, Waggy Tail," purred the cat.

The cat caught a mouse, and they set out for the rich man's house. When they got there, the cat set the mouse down.

"Don't try to trick me," the cat warned. "I know the cat, who lives here, and she is very mean. If you do not get me the ring, I will tell her to eat you."

When the mouse got the ring, she gave it to the cat, who took it between her teeth and started for home, the dog following behind.

Now, the cat could go much faster than the dog. While the dog could only run along the ground, the cat could climb up and jump over everything. So by the time she was home, the dog was still miles behind.

The cat gave the ring to the man and the woman who now felt that their luck had changed.

"Good friend," they said to the cat, "from now on you will live in our house and sleep near the fire."

A few hours later the dog finally arrived home. When the man and woman saw him, they were very angry.

"Where have you been?" they scolded, holding up the lucky ring. "Look what the cat got for us. Why didn't you do something like that for us? Out you go! Sleep in the yard until you learn how to serve us better."

The cat just lay by the fire and purred, but the dog was very angry. The next time the cat came out of the house, he chased her, but she was faster, and still is to this day.

The Blind Men and the Elephant

It was six men of Hindustan
To learning much inclined,
Who went to see the Elephant,
Though all of them were blind,
That each by observation
Might satisfy his mind.

The First approached the Elephant
And, happening to fall
Against his broad and sturdy side,
At once began to bawl:
"God bless me, but the Elephant
Is very like a wall!"

The Second, feeling the tusk,
Cried, "Ho! what have we here,
So very round and smooth and sharp?
To me 'tis very clear
This wonder of an Elephant
Is very like a spear!"

The Third approached the animal
And, happening to take
The squirming trunk within his hands,
Thus boldly up he spake:
"I see," quoth he, "the Elephant
Is very like a snake!"

The Fourth reached out an eager hand
And felt about the knee:
"What most the wondrous beast is like
Is very plain," quoth he.
" 'Tis clear enough the Elephant
Is very like a tree!"

The Fifth, who chanced to touch the ear,
Said, "Even the blindest man
Can tell what this resembles most.
Deny the fact who can:
This marvel of an Elephant
Is very like a fan!"

The Sixth no sooner had begun
About the beast to grope
Than, seizing on the swinging tail
That fell within his scope,
"I see," quoth he, "the Elephant
Is very like a rope!"

And so these men of Hindustan
Disputed loud and long,
Each in his own opinion
Exceeding stiff and strong.
Though each was partly in the right,
They all were in the wrong!

– John Godfrey Saxe

Everything the Lord Does Is for the Best

Each year Rabbi Akiva went to a different town to collect money for the poor students in his care. These young men spent their days studying Torah — the Word of God — and needed charity to live.

On one such trip Rabbi Akiva took some young men with him who had never been as far from home as a mouse wanders from her nest.

The rabbi and his students took with them a donkey to carry the Torah, a candle to study it by, and a rooster to wake them at dawn.

By the time they came to the town, it was dark. They knocked on the gate, but the gatekeeper would not let them in.

"Let us in," cried the students. "It is cold and dark out here. Where are we to sleep?"

"On the ground," said the gatekeeper. "How do I know who you are? You might be robbers."

"But we're honest students."

"Come back in the morning. Then I'll be able to see who you are."

The students began to complain.

"Don't worry," Rabbi Akiva told them. "Everything the Lord does is for the best. Let us find a place to sleep in that nearby field. There will be grass enough for our donkey. We have our candle to study Torah, and our rooster will wake us at dawn."

After finding a place to spend the night, they lit their candle and began to study Torah. But a strong wind blew out the candle, and, try as they might, they could not light it again.

"Good master," complained the students, "how can we study Torah in the dark?"

"Do not fear the dark," their teacher said. "Everything the Lord does is for the best."

A few hours later, the roar of a lion woke them. Then they heard the wild braying of their donkey.

"Silence!" ordered Rabbi Akiva.

Then to their horror, they heard the lion eating their donkey.

"Let us run back to that town!" a student cried.

"Don't be afraid," Rabbi Akiva whispered. "Remember, everything the Lord does is for the best."

Once again they fell asleep but soon awoke in horror. A wildcat was eating their rooster.

"We must run for our lives," they cried.

"Lie back down, my friends, and make no sound," their rabbi whispered.

"But we will be next!"

"The Lord is our Shepherd. He will not forget us in this place of darkness. Remember, everything the Lord does is for the best."

At last, the students fell into a fitful sleep while Rabbi Akiva sat watch.

Night slowly slipped from the sky, and the heavens changed from black to pink to blue. A fresh breeze arose, and soon the good sun gave light and warmth to the world.

"Wake up, my friends," said Rabbi Akiva. "A new day is here, and with it comes another chance to serve the Lord."

As they admired the beautiful morning, a man came running towards them. It was the gatekeeper. He was pale with fear and looked behind him as he ran.

"Why are you running?" they asked.

"Last night a gang of robbers climbed over the walls and stole everyone away. I'm the only one they did not get."

The students gasped in horror.

"Now do you see," said Rabbi Akiva, "how everything the Lord does is for the best? If this gatekeeper had let us in, we would now be slaves. If the donkey and rooster had not been killed, their braying and squawking would have led the robbers to us. And if the candle had not blown out, its light would have led the robbers to us, and now we too would be slaves.

"So do not get too upset by the problems life brings us, my friends. Sometimes a small problem saves you from a problem that is far worse.

"Now, I hope I have taught you at least one thing that you will always remember: Everything the Lord does is for the best."

The Proud Bull-Frog

A big, fat bull-frog was sitting in the mud, bragging to the smaller frogs about his great size.

"Look at me," he bragged. "Am I not the puffiest creature in the world?"

He puffed himself up, and the smaller frogs all agreed that he was puffy indeed. Just then an ox came down to the pond to drink.

"But, Your Puffiness," asked one of the smaller frogs, "is not that ox puffier than you?"

"Humph!" said the bull-frog, and he puffed himself up even more. Soon he was almost twice his size.

"Now, am I not puffier than that mere ox?"

"No, Your Puffiness," they replied. "He's puffier still."

So he **puffed** himself up even more.

"Now I am surely puffier than he!"

"No, your Puffiness. The ox is puffier still."

"Well!" he huffed, and he **puffed** himself up and up until he

BURST!

The Danger of Knowing How to Read

One day, as a fox was trotting through the forest, he met a mule. He had never seen a mule before and felt very afraid. So he turned tail and ran to tell his friend the wolf about the new creature.

"Hmm," said the wolf. "I've never heard of such a creature, but I'm sure it must be good to eat. Let's go and find out."

When they found the mule, the wolf told the fox to go up and ask for its name while he hid in the bushes.

"While you have its attention," said the wolf, "I'll jump on it from behind."

The wolf then slid behind a bush, and the fox went up to the mule.

"Hello, friend," called the fox. "I don't think we've met. I'm a fox. What are you?"

"I got told once," said the mule, "but I done gone an' forgot it. But if you can read, it's writ on my foot."

"Oh," said the fox. "I never learned the art of reading."

The wolf was listening very carefully to what the fox said, and now his vanity was excited, so he stepped out onto the road.

"I know some of that reading stuff," he boasted. "Let me have a look."

The mule lifted his hind foot and said, "It's writ there, on my shoe."

The wolf looked at the nails on the shoe, but he could not make out a thing.

"It's pretty small reading," he said. "I'll have to get a closer look."

The vain wolf then put his nose right up against the mule's hoof. Suddenly, the mule jerked back his leg and kicked the wolf clear over the trees. Seeing what happened to his friend, the fox turned tail and ran.

"Knowing how to read looks pretty bad to me!" said the fox as he ran through the woods. "Who knows what you might learn!"

Lucia and the Trolls

A story to be read aloud by the teacher

A long time ago in a far northern land, at that time of year when darkness has overcome light, and cold has frozen the earth as hard as iron, the trolls would come down from their mountain strongholds and spread fear across the land.

These trolls delighted in wickedness. They pushed huge rocks down the mountainsides. They made great walls of snow slide down into the valleys. They shouted and howled and ran through the villages, smashing whatever they found.

Rotten as the big trolls were, the little ones were worse. One of their nasty tricks was to roll themselves up like logs and hide in woodpiles. Then when some poor human went to fetch wood, the little imps would unroll themselves and laugh horribly. The poor person, needless to say, would cry out in fear, drop the wood, and flee back to his freezing house.

The fear was so great that sometimes even the bravest souls would not even dare to go from house to barn. Who knew what lay in wait for them? Maybe some little troll would jump out from behind a snow pile and scare them. Or maybe even worse. Maybe a big troll would snatch them up and carry them away, high into the mountains, never to be seen again. So the people huddled inside their homes, day after day, while their poor animals, shivering in dark barns, suffered.

One very cold December, the trolls were making more trouble than usual. They had closed off the valleys and blocked all the doors with huge piles of snow. They had released their devil cats who yowled constantly, day and night. So wicked were these trolls that some were even planning to blow out all the fires in the people's homes.

Naturally, everyone was terrified. The old people said they had never known the trolls to act so mean, and the young people swore they would move to the city if spring ever came. It could not have been worse, and the whole village was close to despair.

In a tiny cabin where one distant village nestled against the foot of a great ice field, a family shivered in fear. Hours had passed since their stove had gone cold, and it had been two days since they had eaten their last warm meal. Even though the mother and father were brave souls, they feared that if one of them left to seek help, the trolls would try to snatch their children away.

"Good mother," the good father sighed, "we cannot last much longer. Unless we have food, we will all die. I must go out, no matter how dangerous it is."

He took his strong axe and headed for the door. Outside the trolls howled, and the devil cats yowled, and great rocks crashed down from the mountains. Then just as he touched the door latch, the oldest daughter stood up and declared, "No, Father, I am the one who must go!"

"No, dear child," the father replied. "I am the father and must defend us from this evil. It is my duty."

"Yes, Father, that is true," the brave daughter declared as she stood across the door. "So it is clear that I must be the one to go."

"What do you mean?"

"Once you have gone, father, the trolls will feel bold enough to attack. But if they know that you and Mother are both still inside, our family will be safe. It is clear, I must go."

"She is right," the mother wept, "but how can we let her go?"

The father pondered what to do. Finally he spoke.

"Daughter, take my axe. You are a strong girl, almost a woman. If the trolls come near you, drive them away. They will fear you if you have courage in your heart."

"Thank you, Father," replied the girl, "but you must keep the axe here to defend our family. May the saints protect me. Just give me the lantern, so I can see my way."

Amid much weeping, the brave girl stepped out into the howling dark and held her lantern high. Immediately, the trolls and devil cats saw her. The terrible trolls beat the ground with their clubs, and the cruel devil cats hissed and advanced towards her. But before she could go even one step, a great light filled the darkness. A beautiful maiden stood in the middle of the lane, shining with the glory of Heaven.

The maiden wore a long flowing robe, and, on her head, she wore a wreath of greens, crowned by four bright candles.

Her light shone up to the highest mountain tops and down into deepest caves.

"Never before," the heavenly maiden said with a smile, "has anyone ever dared to venture forth against the trolls. You are the first. Walk with me."

"Who are you?" the girl asked.

"I am Saint Lucia. I light the way."

The sight of this pair amazed the trolls, and they all fell quiet. Even the devil cats stopped their hissing and began to purr, rubbing themselves against the brave girl's legs. Then the little trolls took hands and, singing with joy, began to dance around the brave girl and Saint Lucia.

But most amazing of all, tiny stars danced down from Heaven and came to rest above the little trolls' heads.

One by one, the village doors and windows opened. The sight of the brave girl walking besides the heavenly Saint Lucia filled the villagers with courage and light. Out of their doors they came and gathered around the girl, asking her why she had dared to be so brave and venture out into such danger.

When they learned about her family's hunger, they brought the brave girl trays of warm buns and pots of hot coffee, which she, ever the dutiful daughter, speedily carried home.

So to this day, in the far northern land of Sweden, at that time of year just before Christmas, light overcomes the darkness. It is then that the oldest daughter in every household dresses up like Lucia. Wearing a wreath with candles on her head, she brings warm buns and hot coffee to her home. And while the trolls no longer come down from their mountain strongholds and spread fear across the land, all the little brothers remember them by wearing star-topped hats upon their heads.

Origins of Stories

The Saint Stories:

Godric and the Hare.. Catholic
Saint Moling and the Fox .... Catholic
The Boy Bishop.. Greek Orthodox
The Three Schoolboys and the Salting Tub..... Greek Orthodox
The Three Dowerless Maidens........................ Greek Orthodox
The Golden Cups.. Greek Orthodox
Everything the Lord Does Is for the Best........ Hassidic
A Lesson in Compassion .... Buddhist
Lucia and the Trolls....................................... Sweden/Traditional

The Fables:

The Ant and the Grasshopper .... Aesop
At the Lion's Den .... Aesop
Bell the Cat.. Aesop
The Banyan Deer.. India
The Boy and the Nuts .... Aesop
The Chimp and the Dolphin .... Aesop
The Danger of Knowing How to Read .... Italy
The Dog and the Porcupine........................... West Africa
The Fox in the Grapes .... Aesop
The Frog in the Pail of Cream........................ Aesop
The Gnat and the Lion .... Aesop
The Jackass in the Lion's Skin .... Aesop
The Lion and the Mouse................................. Aesop
The Miller Who Tried to Please Everybody ..... England
The Miser... Aesop
The Proud Bull-Frog .... Aesop
The Turtle Who Talked too Much................... India
Why the Dog and Cat Are Enemies .... China
The Wolf and the Watchdog .... Aesop

Author and Illustrator

Author:

Arthur M. Pittis has been a class and high school humanities teacher in Waldorf schools for twenty-four years, first at the Waldorf School of Baltimore and now at the Austin Waldorf School. He is the author of Pedagogical Theatre *and is a member of the Leadership Council of AWSNA. He is the father of two adult daughters who received Waldorf educations.*

Illustrator:

Ausa M. Peacock attended the Austin Waldorf School from kindergarten through twelfth grade and is currently studying art at Queens University in Kingston, Ontario. In illustrating this series, she called upon her experience as a student in the Waldorf school in creating her warm and evocative drawings.